Mary Pope Osborne

Lex: 240   RL: 2.5   Pts: 3

DATE DUE			
JAN 0 0			
APR 0 0			
MAY 0 0			
SEP 0 0			
OCT 0 0			
NOV 0 0			
NOV 0 0			
JAN 0 1			
MAR 0 1			
MAY 0 1			
GAYLORD 234			PRINTED IN U. S. A.

GAYLORD F

Here's what kids have to say to
Mary Pope Osborne, author of
the Magic Tree House series:

*I wish I could keep all your books in a glass
case with a golden key.*—Luke R.

*I love your books because they are funny
and scary.*—Michael C.

I'd like to be a writer just like you.
—Meghan G.

*I hope you come out with more than one
hundred Jack and Annie books.*—Brock G.

Your books really make me dream.—Kurt K.

*I think you are the best writer in all
mankind!*—Heather O.

Write to Mary Pope Osborne yourself!
See the last page for the address.

Look for these books by
Mary Pope Osborne!

Magic Tree House books:

Dinosaurs Before Dark (#1)
The Knight at Dawn (#2)
Mummies in the Morning (#3)
Pirates Past Noon (#4)
Night of the Ninjas (#5)
Afternoon on the Amazon (#6)
Sunset of the Sabertooth (#7)

Picture books:

Molly and the Prince
Moonhorse

For middle-grade readers:

American Tall Tales
Best Wishes, Joe Brady
Run, Run, as Fast as You Can
*Spider Kane and the Mystery at
    Jumbo Nightcrawler's*
*Spider Kane and the Mystery Under
    the May-Apple*

Magic Tree House #1

Dinosaurs Before Dark

by Mary Pope Osborne

illustrated by Sal Murdocca

Random House  New York

For Linda and Mallory,
who took the trip with me

Library of Congress Cataloging-in-Publication Data
Osborne, Mary Pope. Dinosaurs before dark /
Mary Pope Osborne ; illustrated by Sal Murdocca.   p.   cm. —
(The Magic Tree House)   A First Stepping Stone book
SUMMARY: Eight-year-old Jack and his younger sister Annie find
a magic tree house, which whisks them back to an ancient time zone
where they see live dinosaurs.
ISBN 0-679-82411-1 (trade) — ISBN 0-679-92411-6 (lib. bdg.)
[1. Dinosaurs—Fiction.   2. Time travel—Fiction.
3. Magic—Fiction.   4. Tree houses—Fiction.]
I. Murdocca, Sal, ill.   II. Title.   III. Series.
PZ7.081167Di   1992   [Fic]—dc20   91-51106

Manufactured in the United States of America
19 20

Contents

Dinosaurs
Before Dark

1

Into the Woods

"Help! A monster!" said Annie.

"Yeah, sure," said Jack. "A real monster in Frog Creek, Pennsylvania."

"Run, Jack!" said Annie. She ran up the road.

Oh, brother.

This is what he got for spending time with his seven-year-old sister.

Annie loved pretend stuff. But Jack was eight and a half. He liked *real* things.

"Watch out, Jack! The monster's coming! Race you!"

"No, thanks," said Jack.

Annie raced alone into the woods.

Jack looked at the sky. The sun was about to set.

"Come on, Annie! It's time to go home!"

But Annie had disappeared.

Jack waited.

No Annie.

"Annie!" he shouted again.

"Jack! Jack! Come here!"

Jack groaned. "This better be good," he said.

Jack left the road and headed into the woods. The trees were lit with a golden late-afternoon light.

"Come here!" called Annie.

There she was. Standing under a tall oak tree. "Look," she said. She was pointing at a rope ladder.

The longest rope ladder Jack had ever seen.

"Wow," he whispered.

The ladder went all the way up to the top of the tree.

There—at the top—was a tree house. It was tucked between two branches.

"That must be the highest tree house in the world," said Annie.

"Who built it?" asked Jack. "I've never seen it before."

"I don't know. But I'm going up," said Annie.

"No. We don't know who it belongs to," said Jack.

"Just for a teeny minute," said Annie. She started up the ladder.

"Annie, come back!"

She kept climbing.

Jack sighed. "Annie, it's almost dark. We have to go home."

Annie disappeared inside the tree house.

"An-nie!"

Jack waited a moment. He was about to call again when Annie poked her head out of the tree house window.

"Books!" she shouted.

"What?"

"It's filled with books!"

Oh, man! Jack loved books.

He pushed his glasses into place. He gripped the sides of the rope ladder, and up he went.

2

The Monster

Jack crawled through a hole in the tree house floor.

Wow. The tree house *was* filled with books. Books everywhere. Very old books with dusty covers. New books with shiny, bright covers.

"Look. You can see far, far away," said Annie. She was peering out the tree house window.

Jack looked out the window with her. Down below were the tops of the other trees. In the distance he saw the Frog Creek library.

The elementary school. The park.

Annie pointed in the other direction.

"There's our house," she said.

Sure enough. There was their white wooden house with the green porch. Next door was their neighbor's black dog, Henry. He looked very tiny.

"Hi, Henry!" shouted Annie.

"Shush!" said Jack. "We're not supposed to be up here."

He glanced around the tree house again.

"I wonder who owns all these books," he said. He noticed bookmarks were sticking out of many of them.

"I like this one," said Annie. She held up a book with a castle on the cover.

"Here's a book about Pennsylvania," said Jack. He turned to the page with the book-mark.

"Hey, there's a picture of Frog Creek in here," said Jack. "It's a picture of *these* woods!"

"Oh, here's a book for you," said Annie. She held up a book about dinosaurs. A blue silk bookmark was sticking out of it.

"Let me see it." Jack set down his backpack and grabbed the book from her.

"You look at that one, and I'll look at the one about castles," said Annie.

"No, we better not," said Jack. "We don't know who these books belong to."

But even as he said this, Jack opened the dinosaur book to where the bookmark was. He couldn't help himself.

He turned to a picture of an ancient flying reptile. A Pteranodon.

He touched the huge bat-like wings.

"Wow," whispered Jack. "I wish I could

8

see a Pteranodon for real."

Jack studied the picture of the odd-looking creature soaring through the sky.

"Ahhh!" screamed Annie.

"What?" said Jack.

"A monster!" Annie cried. She pointed to the tree house window.

"Stop pretending, Annie," said Jack.

"No, really!" said Annie.

Jack looked out the window.

A giant creature was gliding above the treetops! He had a long, weird crest on the back of his head. A skinny beak. And huge bat-like wings!

It was a real live Pteranodon!

The creature curved through the sky. He was coming straight toward the tree house. He looked like a glider plane!

The wind began to blow.

The leaves trembled.

Suddenly the creature soared up. High into the sky. Jack nearly fell out the window trying to see it.

The wind picked up. It was whistling now.
The tree house started to spin.
"What's happening?" cried Jack.
"Get down!" shouted Annie.

She pulled him back from the window.

The tree house was spinning. Faster and faster.

Jack squeezed his eyes shut. He held on to Annie.

Then everything was still.

Absolutely still.

Jack opened his eyes. Sunlight slanted through the window.

There was Annie. The books. His backpack.

The tree house was still high up in an oak tree.

But it wasn't the *same* oak tree.

3

Where Is Here?

Jack looked out the window.

He looked down at the picture in the book.

He looked back out the window.

The world outside and the world in the picture—they were exactly the same.

The Pteranodon was soaring through the sky. The ground was covered with ferns and tall grass. There was a winding stream. A sloping hill. And volcanoes in the distance.

"Wh—where are we?" stammered Jack.

The Pteranodon glided down to the base of their tree. The creature coasted to a stop. And stood very still.

"What happened to us?" said Annie. She looked at Jack. He looked at her.

"I don't know," said Jack. "I was looking at the picture in the book—"

"And you said, 'Wow, I wish I could see a Pteranodon for real,'" said Annie.

"Yeah. And then we saw one. In the Frog Creek woods," said Jack.

"Yeah. And then the wind got loud. And the tree house started spinning," said Annie.

"And we landed here," said Jack.

"And we landed here," said Annie.

"So that means . . ." said Jack.

"So that means . . . what?" said Annie.

"Nothing," said Jack. He shook his head. "None of this can be real."

Annie looked out the window again. "But *he's* real," she said. "He's *very* real."

Jack looked out the window with her. The Pteranodon was standing at the base of the oak tree. Like a guard. His giant wings were spread out on either side of him.

"Hi!" Annie shouted.

"Shush!" said Jack. "We're not supposed to be here."

"But where is *here?*" said Annie.

"I don't know," said Jack.

"Hi!" Annie called again to the creature.

The Pteranodon looked up at them.

"Where is *here?*" Annie called down.

"You're nuts. He can't talk," said Jack. "But maybe the book can tell us."

Jack looked down at the book. He read the words under the picture:

> **This flying reptile lived in the Cretaceous period. It vanished 65 million years ago.**

No. Impossible. They couldn't have landed in a time 65 million years ago.

"Jack," said Annie. "He's nice."

"Nice?"

"Yeah, I can tell. Let's go down and talk to him."

"Talk to him?"

Annie started down the rope ladder.

"Hey!" shouted Jack.

But Annie kept going.

"Are you crazy?" Jack called.

Annie dropped to the ground. She stepped boldly up to the ancient creature.

4
Henry

Jack gasped as Annie held out her hand.

Oh, brother. She was always trying to make friends with animals. But this was going too far.

"Don't get too close to him, Annie!" Jack shouted.

But Annie touched the Pteranodon's crest. She stroked his neck. She was talking to him.

What in the world was she saying?

Jack took a deep breath. Okay. He would go down too. It would be good to examine the creature. Take notes. Like a scientist.

Jack started down the rope ladder.

When he got to the ground, Jack was only a few feet away from the creature.

The creature stared at Jack. His eyes were bright and alert.

"He's soft, Jack," said Annie. "He feels like Henry."

Jack snorted. "He's no dog, Annie."

"Feel him, Jack," said Annie.

Jack didn't move.

"Don't think, Jack. Just do it."

Jack stepped forward. He put out his arm. Very cautiously. He brushed his hand down the creature's neck.

Interesting. A thin layer of fuzz covered the Pteranodon's skin.

"Soft, huh?" said Annie.

Jack reached into his backpack and pulled

out a pencil and a notebook. He wrote:

fuzzy skin

"What are you doing?" asked Annie.

"Taking notes," said Jack. "We're probably the first people in the whole world to ever see a real live Pteranodon."

Jack looked at the Pteranodon again. The creature had a bony crest on top of his head. The crest was longer than Jack's arm.

"I wonder how smart he is," Jack said.

"*Very* smart," said Annie.

"Don't count on it," said Jack. "His brain's probably no bigger than a bean."

"No, he's very smart. I can feel it," said Annie. "I'm going to call him Henry."

Jack wrote in his notebook:

small brain?

Jack looked at the creature again. "Maybe he's a mutant," he said.

The creature tilted his head.

Annie laughed. "He's no mutant, Jack."

"Well, what's he doing here then? Where is this place?" said Jack.

Annie leaned close to the Pteranodon.

"Do you know where we are, Henry?" she asked softly.

The creature fixed his eyes on Annie. His long jaws were opening and closing. Like a giant pair of scissors.

"Are you trying to talk to me, Henry?" asked Annie.

"Forget it, Annie." Jack wrote in his notebook:

mouth like scissors?

"Did we come to a time long ago, Henry?"

asked Annie. "Is this a place from long ago?" Suddenly she gasped. "Jack!"

He looked up.

Annie was pointing toward the hill. On top stood a huge dinosaur!

5

Gold in the Grass

"Go! *Go!*" said Jack. He threw his notebook into his pack. He pushed Annie toward the rope ladder.

"Bye, Henry!" she said.

"Go!" said Jack. He gave Annie a big push.

"Quit it!" she said. But she started up the ladder. Jack scrambled after her.

They tumbled into the tree house.

They were panting as they looked out the window at the dinosaur. He was standing on the hilltop. Eating flowers off a tree.

"Oh, man," whispered Jack. "We *are* in a time long ago!"

The dinosaur looked like a huge rhinoceros. Only he had three horns instead of one. Two long ones above his eyes and one on his nose. He had a big shield-like thing behind his head.

"Triceratops!" said Jack.

"Does he eat people?" whispered Annie.

"I'll look it up." Jack grabbed the dinosaur book. He flipped through the pages.

"There!" he said. He pointed to a picture of a Triceratops. He read the caption:

> **The Triceratops lived in the late Cretaceous period. This plant-eating dinosaur weighed over 12,000 pounds.**

Jack slammed the book shut. "Just plants. No meat."

"Let's go see him," said Annie.

"Are you nuts?" said Jack.

"Don't you want to take notes about him?" asked Annie. "We're probably the first people in the whole world to ever see a real live Triceratops."

Jack sighed. She was right.

"Let's go," he said.

He shoved the dinosaur book into his pack. He slung it over his shoulder and started down the ladder.

On the way down, Jack stopped.

He called up to Annie, "Just promise you won't pet him."

"I promise."

"Promise you won't kiss him."

"I promise."

"Promise you won't talk to him."

"I promise."

"Promise you won't—"

"Go! Go!" she said.

Jack went.

Annie followed.

When they stepped off the ladder, the Pteranodon gave them a kind look.

Annie blew a kiss at him. "Be back soon, Henry," she said cheerfully.

"Shush!" said Jack. And he led the way through the ferns. Slowly and carefully.

When he reached the bottom of the hill, he kneeled behind a fat bush.

Annie knelt beside him and started to speak.

"Shush!" Jack put his finger to his lips.

Annie made a face.

Jack peeked out at the Triceratops.

The dinosaur was incredibly big. Bigger than a truck. He was eating the flowers off a magnolia tree.

Jack slipped his notebook out of his pack. He wrote:

eats flowers

Annie nudged him.

Jack ignored her. He studied the Triceratops again. He wrote:

eats slowly

Annie nudged him hard.

Jack looked at her.

Annie pointed to herself. She walked her fingers through the air. She pointed to the dinosaur. She smiled.

Was she teasing?

She waved at Jack.

Jack started to grab her.

She laughed and jumped away. She fell into the grass. In full view of the Triceratops!

"Get back!" whispered Jack.

Too late. The big dinosaur had spotted Annie. He gazed down at her from the hilltop. Half of a magnolia flower was sticking out of his mouth.

"Oops," said Annie.

"Get back!" Jack shouted at her.

"He looks nice, Jack."

"Nice? Watch out for his horns, Annie!"

"No. He's nice, Jack."

Nice?

But the Triceratops just gazed calmly down at Annie. Then he turned and loped away. Down the side of the hill.

"Bye!" said Annie. She turned back to Jack. "See?"

Jack grunted. But he wrote in his notebook:

nice

"Come on. Let's look around some more," said Annie.

As Jack started after Annie, he saw something glittering in the tall grass. He reached out and picked it up.

A medallion. A gold medallion.

A letter was engraved on the medallion. A fancy M.

"Oh, man. Someone came here before us," Jack said softly.

6

Dinosaur Valley

"Annie, look at this!" Jack called. "Look what I found!"

Annie had gone up to the hilltop.

She was busy picking a flower from the magnolia tree.

"Annie, look! A medallion!"

But Annie wasn't paying attention to Jack. She was staring at something on the other side of the hill.

"Oh, wow!" she said.

"Annie!"

Clutching her magnolia flower, she took off down the hill.

"Annie, come back!" Jack shouted.

But Annie had disappeared.

"I'm going to kill her," Jack muttered.

He stuffed the gold medallion into his jeans pocket.

Then he heard Annie shriek.

"Annie?"

Jack heard another sound as well. A deep, bellowing sound. Like a tuba.

"Jack! Come here!" Annie called.

"Annie!"

Jack grabbed his backpack and raced up the hill.

When he got to the top, he gasped.

The valley below was filled with nests. Big nests made out of mud. And the nests were filled with tiny dinosaurs!

Annie was crouching next to one of the nests. And standing over her was a gigantic duck-billed dinosaur!

"Don't panic. Don't move," said Jack. He stepped slowly down the hill toward Annie.

The huge dinosaur was towering above Annie. Waving her arms. Making her tuba sound.

Jack stopped. He didn't want to get too close.

He knelt on the ground. "Okay. Move toward me. Slowly," he said.

Annie started to stand up.

"Don't stand. Crawl," said Jack.

Clutching her flower, Annie crawled toward Jack.

The duck-billed dinosaur followed her. Still bellowing.

Annie froze.

"Keep going," Jack said softly.

Annie started crawling again.

Jack inched farther down the hill. Until he was just an arm's distance from Annie.

He reached out—and grabbed her hand.

He pulled Annie toward him.

"Stay down," he said. He crouched next to her. "Bow your head. Pretend to chew."

"Chew?"

"Yes. I read that's what you do if a mean dog comes at you."

"She's no dog, Jack," said Annie.

"Just chew," said Jack.

Jack and Annie both bowed their heads. And pretended to chew.

Soon the dinosaur grew quiet.

Jack raised his head.

"I don't think she's mad anymore," he said.

"Thanks, Jack, for saving me," said Annie.

"You have to use your brain," said Jack. "You can't just go running to a nest of babies. There's always a mother nearby."

Annie stood up.

"Annie!"

Too late.

Annie held out her magnolia flower to the dinosaur.

"I'm sorry I made you worry about your babies," she said.

The dinosaur moved closer to Annie. She grabbed the flower from her. She reached for another.

"No more," said Annie.

The dinosaur let out a sad tuba sound.

"But there are more flowers up there," Annie said. She pointed to the top of the hill. "I'll get you some."

Annie hurried up the hill.

The dinosaur waddled after her.

Jack quickly examined the babies. Some were crawling out of their nests.

Where were the other mothers?

Jack took out the dinosaur book. He flipped through the pages.

He found a picture of some duck-billed dinosaurs. He read the caption:

The Anatosauruses lived in colonies. While a few mothers baby-sat the nests, others hunted for food.

So there must be more mothers close by.

"Hey, Jack!" Annie called.

Jack looked up. Annie was at the top of the hill. Feeding magnolia flowers to the giant Anatosaurus!

"She's nice, too, Jack," Annie said.

But suddenly the Anatosaurus made her

terrible tuba sound. Annie crouched down
and started to chew.

The dinosaur barged down the hill.

She seemed afraid of something.

Jack put the book down on top of his pack.

He hurried up to Annie.

"I wonder why she ran away," said Annie. "We were starting to be friends."

Jack looked around. What he saw in the distance almost made him throw up.

An enormous ugly monster was coming across the plain.

He was walking on two big legs. And swinging a long, thick tail. And dangling two tiny arms.

He had a huge head. And his jaws were wide open.

Even from far away Jack could see his long, gleaming teeth.

"Tyrannosaurus rex!" whispered Jack.

7

Ready, Set, Go!

"Run, Annie! Run!" cried Jack. "To the tree house!"

They dashed down the hill together. Through the tall grass, through the ferns, past the Pteranodon, and right to the rope ladder.

They scrambled up. Seconds later they tumbled into the tree house.

Annie leaped to the window.

"He's going away!" she said, panting.

Jack pushed his glasses into place. He looked through the window with her.

The Tyrannosaurus was wandering off.

But then the monster stopped and turned around.

"Duck!" said Jack.

The two of them hunched down.

After a long moment, they raised their heads. They peeked out again.

"Coast clear," said Jack.

"Yay," whispered Annie.

"We have to get out of here," said Jack.

"You made a wish before," said Annie.

"I wish we could go back to Frog Creek," said Jack.

Nothing happened.

"I wish—"

"Wait. You were looking at a picture in the dinosaur book. Remember?"

The dinosaur book.

Jack groaned. "Oh, no. I left the book and

my pack on the hill. I have to go back."

"Oh, forget it," said Annie.

"I can't," said Jack. "The book doesn't belong to us. Plus my notebook's in my pack. With all my notes."

"Hurry!" said Annie.

Jack hurried down the rope ladder.

He leaped to the ground.

He raced past the Pteranodon, through the ferns, through the tall grass, and up the hill.

He looked down.

There was his pack, lying on the ground. On top of it was the dinosaur book.

But now the valley below was filled with Anatosauruses. All standing guard around the nests.

Where had they been? Did fear of the Tyrannosaurus send them home?

Jack took a deep breath.

Ready! Set! Go!

He charged down the hill. He leaped to his backpack. He scooped it up. He grabbed the dinosaur book.

A terrible tuba sound! Another! Another! All the Anatosauruses were bellowing at him.

Jack took off.

He raced up to the hilltop.

He started down the hill.

He stopped.

The Tyrannosaurus rex was back! And he was standing between Jack and the tree house!

8

A Giant Shadow

Jack jumped behind the magnolia tree.

His heart was beating so fast he could hardly think.

He peeked out at the giant monster. The horrible-looking creature was opening and closing his huge jaws. His teeth were as big as steak knives.

Don't panic. Think.

Jack peered down at the valley.

Good. The duck-billed dinosaurs were sticking close to their nests.

Jack looked back at the Tyrannosaurus.

Good. The monster still didn't seem to know he was there.

Don't panic. Think. *Think*. Maybe there's information in the book.

Jack opened the dinosaur book. He found Tyrannosaurus rex. He read:

> **Tyrannosaurus rex was the largest meat-eating land animal of all time. If it were alive today, it would eat a human in one bite.**

Great. The book was no help at all.

Okay. He couldn't hide on the other side of the hill. The Anatosauruses might stampede.

Okay. He couldn't run to the tree house. The Tyrannosaurus might run faster.

Okay. Maybe he should just wait. Wait for the monster to leave.

Jack peeked around the tree.

The Tyrannosaurus had wandered *closer* to the hill.

Something caught Jack's eye. Annie was coming down the rope ladder!

Was she nuts? What was she doing?

Jack watched Annie hop off the ladder.

She went straight to the Pteranodon. She was talking to him. She was flapping her arms. She pointed at Jack, at the sky, at the tree house.

She *was* nuts!

"Go! Go back up the tree!" Jack whispered. "Go!"

Suddenly Jack heard a roar.

The Tyrannosaurus rex was looking in his direction.

Jack hit the ground.

The Tyrannosaurus rex was coming toward the hill.

Jack felt the ground shaking.

Should he run? Crawl back into Dinosaur Valley? Climb the magnolia tree?

Just then a giant shadow covered Jack. He looked up.

The Pteranodon was gliding overhead. The giant creature sailed down toward the top of the hill.

He was coming straight for Jack.

9

The Amazing Ride

The Pteranodon coasted down to the ground.

He stared at Jack with his bright, alert eyes.

What was Jack supposed to do? Climb on? "But I'm too heavy," thought Jack.

Don't think. Just do it.

Jack looked at the Tyrannosaurus.

He was starting up the hill. His giant teeth were flashing in the sunlight.

Okay. Don't think. Just do it!

Jack put his book in his pack. Then he eased down onto the Pteranodon's back.

He held on tightly.

The creature moved forward. He spread out his wings—and lifted off the ground!

They teetered this way. Then that.

Jack nearly fell off.

The Pteranodon steadied himself, then rose into the sky.

Jack looked down. The Tyrannosaurus was chomping the air and staring up at him.

The Pteranodon glided away.

He sailed over the hilltop.

He circled over the valley. Over all the nests filled with babies. Over all the giant duck-billed dinosaurs.

Then the Pteranodon soared out over the plain—over the Triceratops who was grazing in the high grass.

It was amazing! It was a miracle!

Jack felt like a bird. As light as a feather.

The wind was rushing through his hair. The air smelled sweet and fresh.

He whooped. He laughed.

Jack couldn't believe it. He was riding on the back of an ancient flying reptile!

The Pteranodon sailed over the stream, over the ferns and bushes.

Then he carried Jack down to the base of the oak tree.

When they came to a stop, Jack slid off the creature's back. And landed on the ground.

Then the Pteranodon took off again and glided into the sky.

"Bye, Henry," whispered Jack.

"Are you okay?" Annie shouted from the tree house.

Jack pushed his glasses into place. He kept staring up at the Pteranodon.

"Jack, are you okay?" Annie called.

Jack looked up at Annie. He smiled.

"Thanks for saving my life," he said. "That was really fun."

"Climb up!" said Annie.

Jack tried to stand. His legs were wobbly.

He felt a bit dizzy.

"Hurry!" shouted Annie. "He's coming!"

Jack looked around. The Tyrannosaurus was heading straight toward him!

Jack bolted to the ladder. He grabbed the sides and started up.

"Hurry! Hurry!" screamed Annie.

Jack scrambled into the tree house.

"He's coming toward the tree!" Annie cried.

Suddenly something slammed against the oak tree. The tree house shook like a leaf.

Jack and Annie tumbled into the books.

"Make a wish!" cried Annie.

"We need the book! The one with the picture of Frog Creek!" said Jack. "Where is it?"

He pushed some books aside. He had to find that book about Pennsylvania.

There it was!

He grabbed it and tore through it, looking for the photograph of the Frog Creek woods.

He found it! Jack pointed to the picture.

"I wish we could go home!" he shouted.

The wind began to moan. Softly at first.

"Hurry!" Jack yelled.

The wind picked up. It was whistling now.

The tree house started to spin.

It spun faster and faster.

Jack closed his eyes. He held on tightly to Annie.

Then everything was still.

Absolutely still.

10

Home Before Dark

A bird began to sing.

Jack opened his eyes. He was still pointing at the picture of the Frog Creek woods.

He peeked out the tree house window. Outside he saw the exact same view.

"We're home," whispered Annie.

The woods were lit with a golden late-afternoon light. The sun was about to set.

No time had passed since they'd left.

"Ja-ack! An-nie!" a voice called from the distance.

"That's Mom," said Annie, pointing.

Jack saw their mother far away. She was
standing in front of their house. She looked
very tiny.

"An-nie! Ja-ack!" she called.

Annie stuck her head out the window and shouted, "Come-ing!"

Jack still felt dazed. He just stared at Annie.

"What happened to us?" he said.

"We took a trip in a magic tree house," said Annie simply.

"But it's the same time as when we left," said Jack.

Annie shrugged.

"And how did it take us so far away?" said Jack. "And so long ago?"

"You just looked at a book and said you wished we could go there," said Annie. "And the magic tree house took us there."

"But *how?*" said Jack. "And who built this magic tree house? Who put all these books here?"

"A magic person, I guess," said Annie.

A magic person?

"Oh, look," said Jack. "I almost forgot about this." He reached into his pocket and pulled out the gold medallion. "Someone lost this back there . . . in dinosaur land. Look, there's a letter M on it."

Annie's eyes got round. "You think *M* stands for *magic person?*" she said.

"I don't know," said Jack. "I just know someone went to that place before us."

"Ja-ack! An-nie!" came the distant cry again.

Annie poked her head out the window. "Come-ing!" she shouted.

Jack put the gold medallion back in his pocket.

He pulled the dinosaur book out of his pack. And put it back with all the other books.

Then he and Annie took one last look around the tree house.

"Good-bye, house," whispered Annie.

Jack slung his backpack over his shoulder. He pointed at the ladder.

Annie started down. Jack followed.

Seconds later they hopped onto the ground and started walking out of the woods.

"No one's going to believe our story," said Jack.

"So let's not tell anyone," said Annie.

"Dad won't believe it," said Jack.

"He'll say it was a dream," said Annie.

"Mom won't believe it," said Jack.

"She'll say it was pretend," said Annie.

"My teacher won't believe it," said Jack.

"She'll say you're nuts," said Annie.

"We better not tell anyone," said Jack.

"I already said that," said Annie.

Jack sighed. "I think I'm starting to not believe it myself," he said.

They left the woods and started up the road toward their house.

As they walked past all the houses on their street, the trip to dinosaur time *did* seem more and more like a dream.

Only *this* world and *this* time seemed real.

Jack reached into his pocket. He clasped the gold medallion.

He felt the engraving of the letter M. It made Jack's fingers tingle.

Jack laughed. Suddenly he felt very happy.

He couldn't explain what had happened today. But he knew for sure that their trip in the magic tree house had been real.

Absolutely real.

"Tomorrow," Jack said softly, "we'll go back to the woods."

"Of course," said Annie.

"And we'll climb up to the tree house," said Jack.

"Of course," said Annie.

"And we'll see what happens next," said Jack.

"Of course," said Annie. "Race you!"

And they took off together, running for home.

Join the
Magic Tree House Club!

Details inside
Magic Tree House #8
Midnight on the Moon
coming to a store near you
in fall 1996!

Where have you traveled in the Magic Tree House?

Check off the Magic Tree House books you have read.

☐ **Magic Tree House #1, Dinosaurs Before Dark,** in which Jack and Annie discover the tree house and travel back to the time of dinosaurs.

☐ **Magic Tree House #2, The Knight at Dawn,** in which Jack and Annie go to the time of knights and explore a medieval castle with a hidden passage.

☐ **Magic Tree House #3, Mummies in the Morning,** in which Jack and Annie go to ancient Egypt and get lost in a pyramid when they help a ghost queen.

☐ **Magic Tree House #4, Pirates Past Noon,** in which Jack and Annie travel back in time and meet some unfriendly pirates searching for buried treasure.

☐ **Magic Tree House #5, Night of the Ninjas,** in which Jack and Annie go to old Japan and learn the secrets of the ninjas.

☐ **Magic Tree House #6, AFTERNOON ON THE AMAZON,** in which Jack and Annie explore the rain forest of the Amazon, and find crocodiles, giant ants, and flesh-eating piranhas.

☐ **Magic Tree House #7, SUNSET OF THE SABERTOOTH,** in which Jack and Annie go back to the Ice Age— the world of woolly mammoths, sabertooth tigers, and a mysterious sorcerer.

COMING IN FALL 1996

Magic Tree House #8, MIDNIGHT ON THE MOON, in which Jack and Annie go forward in time to visit a moon base.

About the Author

Mary Pope Osborne visits schools all over the country and talks to students about her Magic Tree House books. "Kids are a great help to me," she says. "I always get them to vote on where they think Jack and Annie should go. Lots of kids even write their own Magic Tree House stories and share them with me."

If you'd like to share *your* Magic Tree House ideas with Ms. Osborne, you can write to her at this address:

Magic Tree House series

c/o Random House, Inc.

Mail Drop 28-2

201 East 50th Street

New York, NY 10022